BREMEN TOWN MUSICIANS

THE LITTLE RED HEN

HE PRINCESS ON THE PEA

Three Favorite

BOOK CLUB EDITION

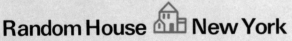

Random House  New York

Copyright © 1975 by Walt Disney Productions. All rights reserved under International and Pan-American Copyright Conventions. Published in the United States by Random House, Inc., New York, and simultaneously in Canada by Random House of Canada Limited, Toronto.
Library of Congress Cataloging in Publication Data
Walt Disney Productions presents Three favorite tales. (Disney's wonderful world of reading, #32) Contents: The Bremen town musicians.—The little red hen.—The princess on the pea. 1. Fairy tales. [1. Fairy tales] I. Grimm, Jakob Ludwig Karl, 1785-1863. Die Bremer Stadtmusikanten. English. 1975. II. Andersen, Hans Christian, 1805-1875. Prindsessen paa aerten. English. 1975. III. Disney (Walt) Productions. IV. Little red hen. 1975.
PZ8.W187   [398.2]   [E]   75-8845
ISBN 0-394-82574-8
ISBN 0-394-92574-2 (lib. bdg.)
Manufactured in the United States of America   1 2 3 4 5 6 7 8 9 0

A B C D E F G H I J K
5 6 7 8 9

B

Tales

BREMEN TOWN MUSICIANS

THE LITTLE RED HEN

PRINCESS ON THE PEA

The Bremen Town Musicians

There was once a poor shoemaker
named Goofy who did not like making shoes.
In fact he hated it.
The only thing he liked to do
was play his tuba.
At last Goofy decided to give up his job.
"I will be a tuba player," he said.
"I will go to Bremen Town
and make music for the king."

On his way to Bremen Town, Goofy met
Farmer Donald planting seeds in a field.
"Work, work, work!" complained Donald.
"I hate working in the fields!"

"Why don't you come with me?" asked Goofy.
"I'm going to Bremen Town to play my tuba
for the king."

"I would like to," said Donald.
"But *I* can't play a tuba."
"You can sing, can't you?" asked Goofy.

"Of course," said Donald.
"Just listen to this.
Qua-qua-qua-quaaaaaack!"

"That sounds good to me,"
said Goofy. "Come along!"

After a long time they came to a broken cart
full of pots and pans.

Beside it sat Peddler Mickey, grumbling.
"I hate this cart! It's always breaking down!"

"Forget your cart," said Goofy. "Come with us."
"Yes," said Donald. "We are going to Bremen Town
to make music for the king."

"That's a good idea!" cried Mickey.
"Some of my pots would make wonderful
drums. I can play *them* for the king!"
"Then come along!" said Goofy.

The musicians walked and walked until dark.
They were feeling tired and hungry.
"I see a light up ahead," said Mickey.
"Let's see if it comes from a house.
Maybe we can get some food there."

Soon Donald cried,
"It *is* a house!"
   "And the light is coming from this window,"
said Goofy.

Goofy was tall.

He could see right into the window.

He could see three mean-looking men.

Piles of gold were lying all around them.

And they were eating a WONDERFUL MEAL!

Goofy turned to his friends and whispered, "There are three men in there. They look like robbers to me. But they have a *lot* of food!"

"Oh, how I would love some of that food!" said Donald.

"I know what we can do," whispered Mickey. And he told them his plan.

Donald climbed on top of Goofy.

Mickey climbed on top of Donald.

Mickey cried, "One . . . two . . . threeeee!"

The three musicians began to sing and play
as loudly as they could.

BANG! BANG! QUA-QUA-QUA-QUAACK!

OOMPAH-PAH! OOMPAH-PAH!

And they tumbled through
the window—CRASH!

The robbers were so scared that they ran
right out of the house.

They ran down the road as fast as they could go.

The musicians wasted no time.

They sat down and finished the robbers' meal.

Donald kept looking at all the gold.

"We are rich!" he cried.

"Now we can go to Bremen Town in style!"

And that's just what they did!

The Little Red Hen

One day the Little Red Hen was raking the yard, and she found a few grains of wheat.

"Who will help me plant this wheat?" she asked.

"Not I," said Huey.
He was too busy
climbing a tree.

"Not I," said Dewey.
He was too busy
playing with his wagon.

"Not I," said Louie.
He was too busy
lying in the sun.

"Then I'll do it myself,"
said the Little Red Hen.

And she did.

Soon the wheat had grown tall.
It was ready to be cut.
"Who will help me cut the wheat?"
the Little Red Hen asked.

"Not I," said Huey,
and he rode off on his
hobby horse.

"Not I," said Dewey,
and he waved from the top
of a tree.

"Not I," said Louie,
and he yawned.

"Then I'll do it myself,"
said the Little Red Hen.

And she did.

Now the wheat was ready to be ground
into flour.

Again the Little Red Hen went to Huey,
Dewey, and Louie.

She asked, "Who will help me carry the wheat
to the mill to be ground?"

"Not I," said Huey.

              "Not I," said Dewey.

                            "Not I," said Louie.

"Then I'll do it myself,"
said the Little Red Hen.

And she did.

When the Little Red Hen came back
from the mill, she asked, "Who will help me
bake this flour into bread?"

Huey was busy taking a nap.
"Not I," he said, half asleep.

Dewey was busy
playing with the pump.
"Not I," he said.

Louie was busy
playing with a toy cart.
"Not I," he said.

"Then I'll do it myself,"
said the Little Red Hen.
And she did.

When the bread came out of the oven,
it smelled *so* good.

"Who will help me eat this bread?"
asked the Little Red Hen.

"I will!" "I will!" "I will!"
cried Huey, Dewey, and Louie.

"Oh, no, you won't!" said the Little Red Hen.
"I planted the grain and cut it.
I carried it to the mill. And I baked it, too.

"Not one of you would help me do the work.
I did it all myself, and now I'll eat the bread
myself!"

And she did.

The Princess on the Pea

Once there was a prince named Mickey.
Since he was a prince,
he wanted to marry a princess.
"But she must be a *real* princess," he said.
He spent many years searching for a real princess.
But he was never able to find one he liked.
So he came home to his parents' castle.

One night a terrible storm was raging.
Rain poured down, and lightning flashed.
Suddenly there was a knock at the castle door.
Mickey's father went to open it.

There stood a stranger dripping wet.
"May I come in?" asked the stranger.
"Of course," said the good king.

"My name is Princess Minnie," the stranger said. "I was out riding and got caught in the storm."

Prince Mickey heard the word "princess," and he came in to see who was there.

Minnie smiled at the prince.

"How handsome he is," she thought.

Mickey smiled back at her.

"How pretty she is," he thought.

"Did you say your name is *Princess* Minnie?"
asked Mickey.

"Yes," said Minnie.

"Are you a real princess?" Mickey asked.

"Of course," said Minnie, nodding her head
and spraying the king with water.

"I hope she *is* a real princess," thought Mickey.

Meanwhile Mickey's mother, the queen,
was listening at the door.

"That wet dishrag doesn't look like a princess
to me," she said. "But we'll soon find out."

The queen went to make up a bed for the princess.
First she put a tiny pea under a thick mattress.

Then she put four more mattresses
on top of the first one.

She kept adding more and more mattresses
to the bed.

"Good," said the queen at last. "Now the pea
is under twenty mattresses. Only a *real*
princess will be able to feel it."

Later that night, Princess Minnie climbed
on top of the twenty mattresses.
She was very tired after
riding so far in the storm.

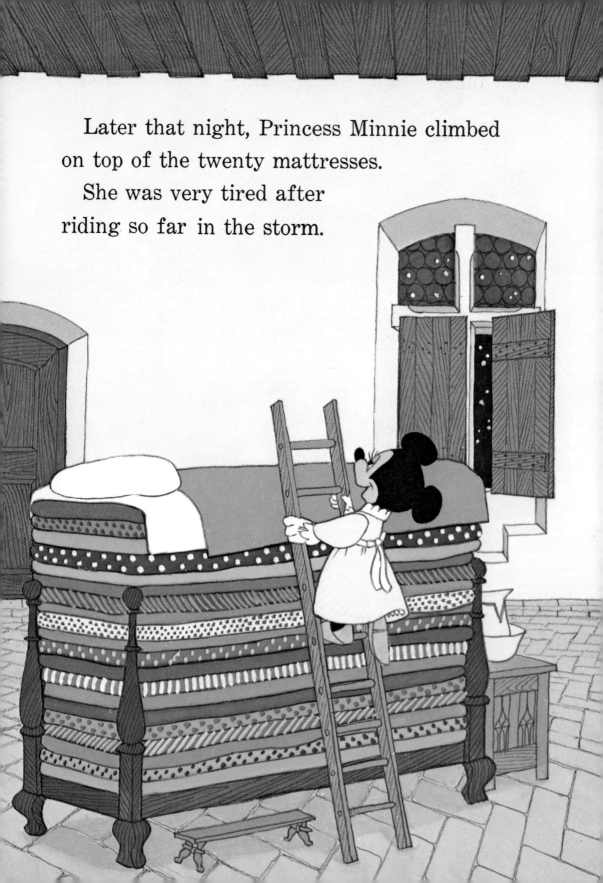

But somehow the bed did not feel comfortable.

Minnie turned on her right side.
But she could not fall asleep.

Then she turned on her left side.
Still she could not fall asleep.

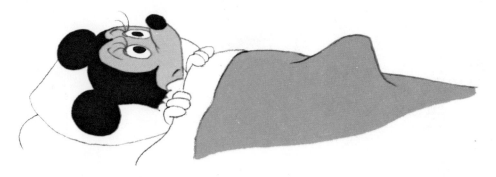

"Maybe flat on my back will be better,"
she thought.
But still, Minnie stayed wide awake.

The next morning Minnie ate breakfast
with the king, the queen, and the prince.
"Did you sleep well?" asked Mickey.

"No," said Minnie, "I did not sleep a wink!
I was lying on something hard, and it kept me awake
all night. I'm quite black and blue all over."

"Then you must be a *real* princess!"
cried the queen. "Only a *real* princess could
have felt that pea."

Prince Mickey had found his *real* princess at last!
So he asked Princess Minnie to be his wife.
Of course she said yes.
They had a real royal wedding
and lived happily ever after.